For George J. – M. W. For Evie – J. L.

First U.S. edition 2004

Library of Congress Cataloging-in-Publication Data is available.

Library of Congress Catalog Card Number 2002035004

ISBN 0-7636-2170-6

2 4 6 8 10 9 7 5 3 1

Printed in China

The illustrations in this book were made from vinyl engravings,
watercolor washes, and printed wood textures. The words were made
from an original alphabet engraved in vinyl. Computer technology was
used to bring these hand-crafted elements together.

Candlewick Press
2067 Massachusetts Avenue
Cambridge, Massachusetts 02140

visit us at www.candlewick.com

PRESS
CHUSETTS

Tiny's Big Adventure

MARTIN WADDELL

illustrated by

JOHN LAWRENCE

Two little mice jumped out
of their hole in the barn.
"I want to go to the wheat field,"
Tiny said.
"I'll take you," said his sister, Katy.
Tiny had never been to the
wheat field before.

The two little mice scampered away through the long grass by the side of the stream. They climbed the knobby tree.

They danced along the top bar of the gate.

They ran down the post and . . .

they were in the wheat field.

They played climb-a-stalk and
you-can't-catch-me-mouse. Then . . .

"What's that, Katy Mouse?"

Tiny whispered. "Is it a cat?"

"It isn't a cat," Katy said.

"It could be," said Tiny.

"It's a rabbit," Katy said. "I know.
I've seen rabbits before."

They played climb-the-tractor and sit-on-the-seat. Tiny tried steering, but the wheel was too big for a small mouse to turn. Then . . .

"What's that, Katy Mouse?"
Tiny asked. "Is it an owl?"
"It's a pheasant," Katy said.
"Owls come out only at night."

They started playing again. Tiny
wanted to play hide-and-seek-mouse.
He ran into the wheat field and hid.

Tiny waited and waited for Katy to come, but he'd run too far, and she couldn't find him.

I'd better go back, Tiny thought.

He ran back through the wheat to find Katy, but . . .

"What's that?"
Tiny said,
and he
quivered.

"What's that?"
Tiny said,
and he
shivered.

"What's THAT?"
Tiny said, and
he shook.
"KATY!"
he called.

And Katy came.

"Thank goodness
    I've found you!"
    said Katy.
"What are those
    scary things,
    Katy Mouse?"
    sobbed Tiny.

"That's a snail," Katy told him. "Look at his shiny bright shell."

"That's a spider," Katy said. "Look at the sun on her web."

"That's a boot!" Katy told Tiny.

"You were lucky to find it!"

They played little-mouse-house in the boot. They played and they played.

Then the two little mice scampered
all the way home.

"That was a big mouse adventure," Tiny said. "Let's do it again, Katy Mouse." And they did.